Robert Seymour Bridges

Ode for the bicentenary commemoration of Henry Purcell

With other poems and a preface on the musical setting of poetry

Robert Seymour Bridges

Ode for the bicentenary commemoration of Henry Purcell
With other poems and a preface on the musical setting of poetry

ISBN/EAN: 9783337111021

Printed in Europe, USA, Canada, Australia, Japan

Cover: Foto ©Andreas Hilbeck / pixelio.de

More available books at **www.hansebooks.com**

Ode to Music

O D E

FOR THE BICENTENARY COMMEMORATION OF HENRY PURCELL, WITH OTHER POEMS AND A PREFACE ON THE MUSICAL SETTING OF POETRY

BY

ROBERT BRIDGES

LONDON
ELKIN MATHEWS, VIGO STREET
1896

PREFACE

THE words of the Ode as here given differ slightly from those which appeared with Dr. Parry's Cantata, sung at the Leeds Festival and at the Purcell Commemoration in London last year.

Since the poem was never perfected as a musical ode,—and I was not in every particular responsible for it,—I have tried to make it more presentable to readers, and in so doing have disregarded somewhat its original intention. But it must still ask indulgence, because it still betrays the liberties and restrictions which seemed to me proper in an attempt to meet the requirements of modern music.

It is a current idea that, by adopting a sort of declamatory treatment, it is possible to give to almost any poem a satisfactory musical setting ;* whence it would follow that a non-literary form is a needless extravagance. From this general condemnation I wish to defend my poem, or rather my judgment, for I do not intend to discuss or defend my poem in detail, nor to try to explain what I hoped to accomplish when I engaged in the work ; it is still further from my intention that anything which I shall say should be taken as applying to the music with which my ode was, far beyond its deserts, honoured and beautified. But I am concerned in combating the general proposition that modern music, by virtue of a declamatory method, is able satisfactorily to interpret almost any kind of good poetry.

Such questions are generally left to the musician, and it should not be unwelcome to hear what may be said on the literary side. I shall therefore state

* For example, there is a passage in Dr. Parry's recent work, " The Art of Music," which will illustrate what I mean. It is in the chapter on Modern Tendencies (see especially p. 311).

what appear to me to be impediments in the way of this announced happy marriage of music and poetry, and enumerate some of the difficulties which, it seems to me, must especially beset the musician, who would attempt to interpret pure literature by musical declamation.

First, the repetitions in music and poetry are incompatible. Though some simple forms dependent on repetition are common to both, yet the general laws are in the two arts contraries. In poetry repetition is avoided, in music it is looked for. A musical phrase has its force and significance increased by repetition, and is often in danger of losing its significance unless it be repeated, whereas such a repetition in poetry is likely to endanger the whole effect of the original statement. And when reiterations that can be compared occur in both, then the second occurrence will in music be generally the strongest, but in poetry the weakest; and the intensity of the repetitions goes on decreasing in music, and increasing for some time in poetry, till both become intolerable.

Secondly, the difficulty which this difference occasions is much heightened by the method of declamatory exposition. Musical declamation must mean that the musical phrase is not chosen, as the earlier musicians might have chosen or invented it, chiefly for the sake of its own musical beauty, in correspondence with the *mood** of the words, and merely fitting the syllables ; but that it is invented also to follow the verbal phrase in correspondence with some notion of rhetorical utterance, or natural inflection

---

* I omit the *idea*, the musical suggestion of which is a feat of genius, independent of style. The apprehension and exhibition of the *mood* is generally considered a simple matter, but really it affords a wide field for subtlety of interpretation. I have, for the sake of simplicity, assumed that in their choral music the older musicians altogether disregarded the speech inflexion of the *phrase* : but this is not quite true, and since, especially in such words as they usually set, the speech inflexion is often uncertain and unimportant, or altogether a nonentity, and would very well correspond with almost any simple musical expression of the mood, this distinction between ancients and moderns cannot always be seen, or will appear only as a difference of degree.

of speech enforcing the sense, and in so far with lesser regard to its own purely musical value. Such a musical phrase will therefore, in proportion to its success, be more closely associated with the words, and cannot well be repeated unless the words are repeated, which the declamation forbids.

Thirdly, when a declamatory musical movement is once started, the musician has very few means of bringing it to a conclusion. There is the method of repetition, which does not suit the Ode,* and which on his own theory he is almost forbidden to use; and there is the method of rising to a climax, which is perhaps the most usual device: but few poems can offer occasion for the recurrence of climax, and its employment would break up an ode into artificial sections, which the poet must

* Throughout these remarks I speak chiefly of the Ode. It is necessary in so wide a subject to aim at a definite mark, and while an ode happens to be in question, the Ode is also the example which is taken by Dr. Parry in the passage to which I have referred the reader.

repudiate.   In pure music the musician
has invented many beautiful devices, but
in choral music he has not yet shown,
so far as I know, any power to match
the poet's liberty in this respect, whose
resources are as various as numerous,
and are comparable to the freedom and
caprices of a dancer, who can at any
moment surprise by a gesture and be
still.

Fourthly, the very rhythms of poetry
and choral music are different in kind.
The rhythms and balances of verse are
unbarred, the rhythms of choral music
are barred.   Even the universally recognised fitness of the interpretation of a
common measure in verse by the cor-
responding common measure in music
depends much more on the power and
satisfying completeness of the musical
form in itself than on any right relation
which obtains between words and music
under these conditions.   Where the poetry
has a more elaborated rhythm there are
two extremes, between which the musician's manner of setting must lie.   One

extreme, the musical, is that he should disregard the poetic rhythm for the sake of new musical ideas, which must of course add beauty and not do violence to the words : the other is that he should follow the elaborate poetic rhythm as nearly as possible. The method of declamation takes this latter extreme; it forbids musical independence, and prefers so identify itself with the poetic rhythm, which in good poetry represents an ideal cadence of speech : but this interpretation is really a convention and a make-believe, and at best only an ingenious translation ; and though it may often be desirable, and the occasion of true musical beauty, yet its exclusive use is an abnegation of musical spontaneity for the sake of a secondary, mediate form, conspicuously dependent on something extraneous ; it gives prominence to ingenuity rather than to pure æsthetic beauty, and must provoke criticism rather than unquestioning delight.

Fifthly, the most beautiful effects in poetry are obtained by suggestion. A

certain disposition of ideas in words pro-
duces a whole result quite out of proportion to the parts : and if it is asked what
music can do best, it is something in
this same way of indefinite suggestion.
Poetry is here the stronger, in that its
suggestion is more definitely directed.
Music is the stronger in the greater force
of the emotion raised.   It would seem
therefore that music could have no more
fit and congenial task than to heighten
the emotion of some great poetic beauty,
the direction of which is supplied by the
words.   But if it seeks to do this by
a method of declamation, it commits a
double mistake.   First it tries to en-
force the poetic means, which it may be
assumed are already on full strain, and
in exact balance, and will not bear the
least disturbance ; and secondly it re-
nounces its own highest power of stirring
emotion, because that resides in pure
musical beauty, and is dependent on its
mysterious quality ; for one may say that
its power is in proportion to its remote-
ness from common direct understanding,

and that just in so far as its sounds are understood to mean something definite, they lose their highest emotional power. It would follow from this that the best musical treatment of passages of great poetic beauty is not to declaim them, but, as it were, to woo them and court them and caress them, and deck them with fresh musical beauties ; approaching them tenderly now on one side, now on another, and to keep a delicate reserve which shall leave their proper unity unmolested.

Sixthly, if this is true of the highest poetic beauty, how will the declamatory method fare when it has to deal with the commonplaces and bare or even ugly words which are the weaknesses and unkindnesses of language ? Just when the poet must deplore that his material is not more musical, it cannot be the musician's triumph to insist on the defect. The ordinary monosyllabic exclamations are a sufficient example ; there is absolutely no declamatory rendering of these, which is at all worthy of the emotion which they must often be employed to convey. What can be made of them by a purely musical treatment is seen in the long-drawn melodious sighs with which Carissimi or Purcell interpreted the Ohs and Ahs.

Seventhly, this leads to the more general remark that the inflexions of all speech are much more limited in character, number and scope than those of the trained singing voice. Whence it comes that the imitations of speech in declamatory music have a tendency to fall into a comparatively small number of forms, which, even when most skilfully disguised, are easily recognised by an attentive ear, and soon weary with their sameness. The basis of declamatory music is in fact no broader than that of the old *recitativo secco*, and it would seem unreasonable to hope that any ingenuity in the superstructure can long disguise this, or save itself ultimately from the same condemnation.

Eighthly, in consideration of the commonest difficulties which arise in setting

to music words which have not been
specially contrived for it, it appears that,
compared with a more purely musical
way, the declamatory method is absolutely at a disadvantage.   It can do
nothing with parentheses or dependent
clauses.   The weak polysyllables, which
have fit place in the diction and rhythm
of verse, may be helped out by convention or by pure musical distraction, but
declamation can only make them ugly.
And as those for their weakness of
sound, so other words unable for their
sense to bear the stress of singing,—
such as metaphorical words of slight
meaning, which in poetry contribute but
a part of themselves to the main idea,—
these declamation would make ridiculous.
Nor on the other hand, with the words
and phrases which are generally held
most suitable for music, is the declamatory method any richer or happier: these
are the well-sounding words of broad
meaning, and their common collocations;
which require a fresh imagination to
revivify them.   But the musician was

always at his ease with these words, because his music was free to adorn them with any quantity of enrichment ; and this commanded the attention the more completely when the words required none. Now if they are to be declaimed, they must return to their old prosaic nakedness ; and since the attention is to be called to them, they will be even worse off than ever.

The above remarks are sufficient for my purpose : but so many negations may provoke the reader to look for some positive indication of the writer's opinion as to what sort of words are best suited for music, and what sort of setting they should have. This question is far too wide to be treated summarily, and if it has not been given to me to assist in solving it practically, I cannot venture to meddle with it further. I had hoped, as a matter of fact, to contrive something ; but it seems to me that the musician's difficulty in advancing towards a solution is much increased by the necessity of pleasing large audiences.

It is certain that the final appeal is not to the first hearing of any large audience in this country. What sort of music is really in request may be judged from the repertories of our military bands, and the programmes of the Royal concerts. Even the highest class concerts I have seen interlarded with unworthy items, which were rapturously received by the fashionable hearers who did not recognise the trap.

> The man that hath no music in himself
> Is fit for treasons, stratagems and spoils.

and these were the stratagems to obtain his spoils.

It is possible enough that an audience may enjoy having commonplaces vociferated at them with orchestral accompaniment : but this is nothing. To the musician the poet will say that he is surprised to find a term, which is considered a reproach in poetry, esteemed as the expression of the best means of its interpretation. To call a poem declamatory or rhetorical is to condemn it : and music is naturally less rhetorical than

B

speech, so that in a declamatory interpretation of poetry music would seem to abnegate its own excellence for the sake of a quality foreign to itself and repudiated by the art which it is seeking to heighten.

He will not be satisfied by the assurance that the method will serve to introduce and explain poetry to some people who are generally indifferent to it : it will seem to him that the musician is labouring to introduce into pure vocal music the old dramatic crux, that awkwardness from which it has, in its best forms been beautifully free.   Because in the musical drama that must be sung which should be spoken, why try to make that seem to be spoken which should be sung?

ANALYSIS OF ODE

This analysis is taken from the concert programme

I. An invitation to Music to return to England: that is, in the sense that England should be again pre-eminent for music above other European nations, as she was in the 16th century. The three English Graces are Liberty, Poetry and Music.

II. Music invited in the name of Liberty: the idea associated with the forest.

III. Music invited in the name of Poetry: the idea of Poetry associated with pastoral scenes and husbandry.

IV. The Sea introduced as the type of Love; isolating our Patriotism, and making our bond with the rest of the world.

V. The national intention gives way to wider human sympathies. Music here considered as the voice of Universal Love, calling and responding throughout the world.   A national meaning also underlies, in respect of our world-wide colonisation.

VI. Sorrow now invites Music; asserting her need to be the chiefest.   The occasion being the celebration of Purcell's genius, her complaint implies a call for some musical lament for his untimely death.

VII. Music replies with a dirge for the dead artist ; offering no consolation beyond the expression of woe.

VIII. The chorus consoled praise dead artists, and pronounce them happy and immortal.

IX. A picture of the ideal world of delight created by Art.

X. The invocation repeated, with the idea of responsibility of our colonisation.

Ode to Music

WRITTEN FOR THE BICENTENARY
COMMEMORATION OF

HENRY PURCELL

I

MYRIAD-VOICED Queen, Enchantress of the air,
Bride of the life of man!   With tuneful reed,
With string and horn and high-adoring quire
Thy welcome we prepare.
In silver-speaking mirrors of desire,
In joyous ravishment of mystery draw thou near,
With heavenly echo of thoughts, that dreaming
        lie
Chain'd in unborn oblivion drear,
Thy many-hearted grace restore
Unto our isle our own to be,
And make again our Graces three.

II

Turn, O return!   In merry England
Foster'd thou wert with infant Liberty.
Her hallow oaks, that stand
With trembling leaves and giant heart
Drinking in beauty from the summer moon,
Her wild-wood once was dear to thee.

There the birds with tiny art
Earth's immemorial cradle tune
Warble at dawn to fern and fawn,
In the budding thickets making merry;
And for their love the primrose faint
Floods the green shade with youthful scent.

Come, thy jocund spring renew
By hyacinthine lakes of blue:
Thy beauty shall enchant the buxom May;
And all the summer months shall strew thy way,
And rose and honeysuckle rear
Their flowery screens, till under fruit and berry
The tall brake groweth golden with the year.

III

Thee fair Poetry oft hath sought,
Wandering lone in wayward thought,
On level meads by gliding streams,
When summer noon is full of dreams :
And thy loved airs her soul invade,
Haunting retired the willow shade.

Or in some wallèd orchard nook
She communes with her ancient book,
Beneath the branches laden low ;
While the high sun o'er bosom'd snow
Smiteth all day the long hill-side,
With ripening cornfields waving wide.

There if thou linger all the year,
No jar of man can reach thine ear,
Or sweetly comes, as when the sound
From hidden villages around,
Threading the woody knolls, is borne
Of bells that dong the Sabbath morn.

IV

1

The sea with melancholy war
Moateth about our castled shore;
His world-wide elemental moan
Girdeth our lives with tragic zone.

He, ere men dared his watery path,
Fenced them aloof in wrath;
Their jealous brotherhoods
Sund'ring with bitter floods:
Till science grew and skill,
And their adventurous will
Challenged his boundaries, and went free
To know the round world, and the sea
From midday night to midnight sun
Binding all nations into one.

2

Yet shall his storm and mastering wave
Assure the empire to the brave;
And to his billowy bass belongs
The music of our patriot songs,

When to the wind his ridges go
In furious following, careering a-row,
Lasht with hail and withering snow:
And ever undaunted hearts outride
   His rushing waters wide.

3

   But when the winds fatigued or fled
Have left the drooping barks unsped,
And nothing stirs his idle plain
Save fire-breathed ships with silvery train,
While lovingly his waves he layeth,
And his slow heart in passion swells
To the pale moon in heav'n that strayeth,
And all his mighty music deep
Whispers among the heapèd shells,
Or in dark caverns lies asleep;—
   Then dreams of Peace invite,
Haunting our shore with kisses light:
Nay—even Love's Paphian Queen hath come
Out of her long-retirèd home
To show again her beauty bright;
And twice or thrice in sight hath play'd
Of a young lover unaffray'd,
And all his verse immortal made.

V

1

Love to Love calleth,
Love unto Love replieth:
From the ends of the earth, drawn by invisible
    bands,
Over the dawning and darkening lands
    Love cometh to Love.

    To the pangs of desire;
To the heart by courage and might
Escaped from hell,
From the torment of raging fire,
From the sighs of the drowning main,
From shipwreck of fear and pain,
From the terror of night.

2

All mankind by Love shall be banded
To combat Evil, the many-handed:
For the spirit of man on beauty feedeth,
The airy fancy he heedeth,

He regardeth Truth in the heavenly height,
In changeful pavilions of loveliness dight,
The sovran sun that knows not the night ;
He loveth the beauty of earth,
And the sweet birds' mirth ;
And out of his heart there falleth
A melody-making river
Of passion, that runneth ever
To the ends of the earth and crieth,
That yearneth and calleth ;
And Love from the heart of man
To the heart of man replieth :
      On the wings of desire
      Love cometh to Love.

VI

1

To me, to me, fair hearted Goddess, come,
     To Sorrow come,
Where by the grave I linger dumb;
    With sorrow bow thine head
    For all my beauty is dead.
Leave Freedom's vaunt and playful thought awhile,
Come with thine unimpassioned smile
Of heavenly peace, and with thy fourfold choir
    Of fair uncloying harmony
Unveil the palaces where man's desire
Keepeth celestial solemnity.

2

Lament, fair hearted queen, lament with me:
For when thy seer died no song was sung,
Nor for our heroes fal'n by land or sea
    Hath honour found a tongue:
Nor aught of beauty for their tomb can frame
    Worthy their noble name.
Let Mirth go bare: make mute thy dancing string:

With thy majestic consolation
Sweeten our suffering.
Speak thou my woe; that from her pain
My spirit arise to see again
The Truth unknown that keeps our faith,
The Beauty unseen that bates our breath,
The heaven that doth our joy renew,
And drinketh up our tears as dew.

VII

DIRGE

Man born of desire
Cometh out of the night,
A wandering spark of fire
A lonely word of eternal thought
Echoing in chance and forgot.

I

He seeth the sun,
He calleth the stars by name,
He saluteth the flowers.—
Wonders of land and sea,
The mountain towers
Of ice and air
He seeth, and calleth them fair:
    Then he hideth his face;—
Whence he came to pass away
Where all is forgot,
Unmade—lost for aye
With the things that are not.

2

He striveth to know,
To unravel the Mind
That veileth in horror:
He wills to adore.
In wisdom he walketh
And loveth his kind;
His labouring breath
Would keep evermore:
    Then he hideth his face;—
Whence he came to pass away
Where all is forgot,
Unmade—lost for aye
With the things that are not.

3

He dreameth of beauty,
He seeks to create
Fairer and fairer
To vanquish his Fate;
No hindrance he
No curse will brook,
He maketh a law
No ill shall be:
    Then he hideth his face;—
Whence he came to pass away
Where all is forgot,
Unmade—lost for aye
With the things that are not.

VIII

Rejoice, ye dead, where'er your spirits dwell,
Rejoice that yet on earth your fame is bright,
And that your names, remembered day and night,
Live on the lips of those who love you well.
  'Tis ye that conquer'd have the powers of Hell
Each with the special grace of your delight;
Ye are the world's creators, and by might
Alone of Heavenly love ye did excel.

Now ye are starry names
Behind the sun ye climb
To light the glooms of Time
  With deathless flames.

IX

Open for me the gates of delight,
The gates of the garden of man's desire;
Where spirits touched by heavenly fire
   Have planted the trees of life.—
Their branches in beauty are spread,
     Their fruit divine
To the nations is given for bread,
   And crushed into wine.

To thee, O man, the sun his truth hath given;
The moon hath whisper'd in love her silvery
     dreams;
Night hath unlockt the starry heaven,
The sea the trust of his streams:
And the rapture of woodland spring
    Is stay'd in its flying;
    And Death cannot sting
    Its beauty undying.

Fear and Pity disentwine
Their aching beams in colours fine;
Pain and woe forego their might.
After darkness thy leaping sight,
After dumbness thy dancing sound,
After fainting thy heavenly flight,
After sorrow thy pleasure crowned:
O enter the garden of thy delight,
    Thy solace is found.

X

To us, O Queen of sinless grace,
Now at our prayer unveil thy face:
Awake again thy beauty free;
Return and make our Graces three.
And with our thronging strength to the ends of
        the earth
Thy myriad-voicèd loveliness go forth,
    To lead o'er all the world's wide ways
        God's everlasting praise,
        And every heart inspire
With the joy of man in the beauty of Love's desire.

FINIS

An effigy of brass
Trodden by careless feet
Of worshippers that pass,
Beautiful and complete,

Lieth in the sombre aisle
Of this old church unwreckt,
And still from modern style
Shielded by kind neglect.

It shows a warrior arm'd:
Across his iron breast
His hands by death are charmed
To leave his sword at rest,

Wherewith he led his men
O'ersea, and smote to hell
The astonisht Saracen,
Nor doubted he did well.

Would we could teach our sons
His trust in face of doom,
Or give our bravest ones
A comparable tomb:

Such as to look on shrives
The heart of half its care;
So in each line survives
The spirit that made it fair,

So fair the characters,
With which the dusty scroll,
That tells his title, stirs
A requiem for his soul.

Yet dearer far to me,
And brave as he are they,
Who fight by land and sea
For England at this day;

Whose vile memorials,
In mournful marbles gilt,
Deface the beauteous walls
By growing glory built.

Heirs of our antique shrines,
Sires of our future fame,
Whose starry honour shines
In many a noble name

Across the deathful days,
Link'd in the brotherhood
That loves our country's praise,
And lives for heavenly good.

NOVEMBER

I

THE lonely season in lonely lands, when fled
Are half the birds, and mists lie low, and the sun
Is rarely seen, nor strayeth far from his bed;
The short days pass unwelcomed one by one.

Out by the ricks the mantled engine stands
Crestfallen, deserted,—for now all hands
Are told to the plough,—and ere it it is dawn
    appear
The teams following and crossing far and near,
As hour by hour they broaden the brown bands
Of the striped fields; and behind them firk and
    prance
The heavy rooks, and daws grey-pated dance:
Or awhile, surmounting a crest against the sky,
Pictured a whole team stands, or now near by
Above the lane they shout lifting the share,
By the trim hedgerow bloom'd with purple air;
Where, under the thorns, dead leaves in huddle lie
Packed by the gales of Autumn, and in and out
The small wrens glide
With a happy note of cheer,
And yellow amorets flutter above and about,
Gay, familiar in fear.

2

And now, if the night shall be cold, across the sky
Linnets and twites, in small flocks helter-skelter,
All the afternoon to the gardens fly,
From thistle-pastures hurrying to gain the shelter
Of American rhododendron or cherry-laurel:
And here and there, near chilly setting of sun,
In an isolated tree a congregation
Of starlings chatter and chide,
Thickset as summer leaves, in garrulous quarrel:
Suddenly they hush as one,—
The tree top springs,—
And off, with a whirr of wings,
They fly by the score
To the holly-thicket, and there with myriads more
Dispute for the roosts; and from the unseen nation
A babel of tongues, like running water unceasing,
Makes live the wood, the flocking cries increasing,
Wrangling discordantly, incessantly,
While falls the night on them self-occupied;
The long dark night, that lengthens slow,
Deepening with Winter to starve grass and tree,
And soon to bury in snow
The Earth, that, sleeping 'neath her frozen stole,
Shall dream a dream crept from the sunless pole
Of how her end shall be.

THE SOUTH WIND

1

THE south wind rose at dusk of the winter day,
The warm breath of the western sea
Circling wrapp'd the isle with his cloke of cloud,
And it now reach'd even to me, at dusk of the day,
And moan'd in the branches aloud:
While here and there, in patches of dark space,
A star shone forth from its heavenly place,
As a spark that is borne in the smoky chase;
· And, looking up, there fell on my face—
Could it be drops of rain
Soft as the wind, that fell on my face?
Gossamers light as threads of the summer dawn,
Suck'd by the sun from midmost calms of the main,
From groves of coral islands secretly drawn,
O'er half the round of earth to be driven,
Now to fall on my face
In silky skeins spun from the mists of heaven.

2

Who art thou, in wind and darkness and soft
      rain
Thyself that robest, that bendest in sighing pines

To whisper thy truth? that usest for signs
A hurried glimpse of the moon, the glance of a
    star
In the rifted sky?
Who art thou, that with thee I
Woo and am wooed?
That robing thyself in darkness and soft rain
Choosest my chosen solitude,
Coming so far
To tell thy secret again,
As a mother her child, in her folding arm
Of a winter night by a flickering fire,
Telleth the same tale o'er and o'er
With gentle voice, and I never tire,
So imperceptibly changeth thy charm,
As Love on buried ecstasy buildeth his tower,
—Like as the stem that beareth the flower
By trembling is knit to power ;—
Ah! long ago
In thy first rapture I renounced my lot,
The vanity, the despondency and the woe,
And seeking thee to know
Well was't for me, and evermore
I am thine, I know not what.

3

    For me thou seekest ever, me wondering a day
In the eternal alternations, me

Free for a stolen moment of chance
To dream a beautiful dream
In the everlasting dance
Of speechless worlds, the unsearchable scheme,
To me thou findest the way,
Me and whomsoe'er
I have found my dream to share
Still with thy charm encircling; even to-night
To me and my love in darkness and soft rain
Under the sighing pines thou comest again,
And staying our speech with mystery of delight,
Of the kiss that I give a wonder thou makest,
And the kiss that I take thou takest.

THE day begins to droop,—
   Its course is done:
But nothing tells the place
   Of the setting sun.

The hazy darkness deepens,
   And up the lane
You may hear, but cannot see,
   The homing wain.

An engine pants and hums
   In the farm hard by:
Its lowering smoke is lost
   In the lowering sky.

The soaking branches drip,
   And all night through
The dropping will not cease
   In the avenue.

A tall man there in the house
   Must keep his chair:
He knows he will never again
   Breathe the spring air:

His heart is worn with work;
   He is giddy and sick
If he rise to go as far
   As the nearest rick:

He thinks of his morn of life,
   His hale, strong years;
And braves as he may the night
   Of darkness and tears.

FINIS

NOTES.—On p. 22, *line* 9. Fern and fawn *is from* Sidney Lanier.—*P.* 26, *line* 9. Fire *is passion. Line* 10. *Is pity.—P.* 28, *2nd stanza. The meaning here having been mistaken by critics, I have put next after the Ode, a poem called* "The Fair Brass," *which deals with the same idea.—P.* 32. *The four first lines are from* "The Growth of Love."—*P.* 39. The South Wind. *This Poem appeared in* The Pageant, *Christmas,* 1895.

R.B.   1896.